KT-460-839

Cardiff Libraries
www.cardiff.gov.uk/libraries
Llyfrgelloedd Caerdydd
www.caerdydd.gov.uk/llyfrgelloedd

THE SECRET SEVEN

Good Old Secret Seven

ACC. No: 03177562

Have you read them all?

Enid Blyton

THE SECRET SEVEN

Good Old Secret Seven

ILLUSTRATED BY Tony Ross

Hodder
Children's
Books

A division of Hachette Children's Books

Text copyright © Hodder & Stoughton Ltd
Illustrations copyright © Tony Ross

First published in Great Britain in 1960 by Hodder & Stoughton Ltd
This edition published in 2013

The rights of Enid Blyton and Tony Ross to be identified as the Author
and Illustrator of the Work respectively have been asserted by them in
accordance with the Copyright, Designs and Patents Act 1988

2

All rights reserved. Apart from any use permitted under UK copyright law,
this publication may only be reproduced, stored or transmitted, in any form,
or by any means with prior permission in writing from the publishers or in
the case of reprographic production in accordance with the terms of licences
issued by the Copyright Licensing Agency and may not be otherwise circulated
in any form of binding or cover other than that in which it is published and
without a similar condition being imposed on the subsequent purchaser.

All characters in this publication are fictitious and any resemblance
to real persons, living or dead, is purely coincidental.

A Catalogue record for this book is available from the British Library

ISBN 978 1 44491354 5

Typeset by Hewer Text UK Ltd, Edinburgh
Printed and bound in Great Britain by Clays Ltd, St Ives plc

The paper and board used in this paperback by Hodder Children's Books are natural
recyclable products made from wood grown in sustainable forests. The manufacturing
processes conform to the environmental regulations of the country of origin.

Hodder Children's Books
a division of Hachette Children's Books
338 Euston Road, London NW1 3BH
An Hachette UK company

www.hodderchildrens.co.uk

CONTENTS

CHAPTER ONE

A MEETING IS CALLED

ONE MORNING after school, Peter went to find his sister Janet.

'Hey, Janet!' he called. 'I'm calling a Secret Seven meeting for tomorrow morning. Jack's uncle has given him a super present, and he wants all the Seven to share it.'

'What is it?' asked Janet. 'A game of some sort?'

'No. You'll have to wait and see,' said Peter. 'It's Jack's surprise, not mine. Will you write out a few notes and tell the others to come – ten o'clock sharp. Thank goodness it's Saturday tomorrow.'

'Wuff,' said Scamper the spaniel. He loved Saturdays too. He knew he would have Peter and Janet all day long then.

'Yes, *you* shall come to the meeting as well,' said Janet, patting his soft golden coat. 'But do you know the password, Scamper?'

'Wuff-wuff!' said Scamper at once, and the children laughed.

'Quite right – the password *is* "wuff-wuff",' said Peter. 'What a good memory you have, Scamper!'

Scamper wagged his tail, and said 'wuff-wuff' again. 'Better not say it too often, Scamper,' said Janet. 'Or that awful Susie might hear you.'

Susie was Jack's sister, and *not* one of the Secret Seven, though she badly wanted to belong. She loved to find out whatever password the Secret Seven were using, and it really was quite difficult to stop her.

Janet scribbled four cards – one to Colin, one to George, one to Pam and one to Barbara. 'There!' she said, 'I'll take them round on my bike. I don't need to write to Jack, as he's asked for the meeting himself. Is he going to bring this present of his tomorrow, whatever it is?'

A MEETING IS CALLED

'Yes,' said Peter. 'I'd better tidy up the shed where we meet – and I'll ask Mother what she can spare for us to eat. I *think* she is baking today, so perhaps there'll be something special!'

Next morning Janet and Peter went down to their shed at a quarter to ten, carrying a good many things. 'I've tidied it up,' said Peter. 'The gardener had been in and taken two of the big flowerpots we used as seats, but I found two boxes instead.'

The shed-door had on it the two big letters S.S., standing for Secret Seven. Janet and Peter looked at them proudly.

'Secret Seven!' said Janet. 'Best club in the world! I *shall* enjoy a meeting again – it's weeks since we had one – we've been so busy with school things.'

In they went, and shut the door. Now no one would be allowed in unless they gave the password. Peter set down the things he was carrying, and looked round proudly. 'Didn't I clean the shed well?' he said. 'I even cleaned the windows. It's nice and warm too, isn't it?'

The shed backed on to the hot greenhouse, and so gained some of the heat from there. It was pleasantly warm on this cold November day. Janet began to set out some coloured mugs, taking them down from the shelf.

'Mother thought we'd better have hot cocoa this cold day,' she said. 'I'll fetch it as soon as everyone is here. I bet Jack will be first with his wonderful present, whatever it is! Where's Scamper?'

'I don't know. He didn't come down with us. I expect he'll turn up,' said Peter. 'He's probably chasing his old enemy – the stable cat. He *still* thinks he can catch her, though he never will.'

'Look what Mother's given us,' said Janet, showing Peter a tin full of buns. 'Currant buns warm from the oven – and a home-made macaroon for each of us!'

A MEETING IS CALLED

'Good old Mother!' said Peter, sniffing at the warm buns. 'One of these days I'll buy her a medal. Hurry up, Janet – the others will be here in half a minute. I hope they'll all remember the password! Listen – here comes the first one. I bet it's Jack.'

CHAPTER TWO

THAT AWFUL SUSIE!

A FIST banged on the door, and Peter called out at once. 'Password, please.'

'Wuff-wuff!' said a voice, rather loudly.

'Enter,' said Peter, 'and DO remember not to say the password so that everyone can hear it for a mile around!'

'Sorry!' said George, coming in at the door, a grin on his face. 'Did I sound like Scamper? I tried to.'

'Well, you didn't,' said Janet. 'You sounded exactly like yourself. Sit down, George. We thought you were Jack. He said he'd be here early, because he has something to show us.'

Knock-knock – somebody else had come. 'Password!' yelled Peter, and the answer came at once. 'Wuff-wuff! Wuff-wuff!'

In came Pam and Barbara, beaming all over their faces. 'Hello! We're not the last. Good!'

Bang-bang! '*That* must be Jack,' said Janet, as Peter called out 'Password, please!' But it wasn't. It was Colin. He marched in and shut the door smartly. 'Hallo, everyone! I say, it's nice and warm in here! What's the meeting called for? Anything special?'

'Yes,' said Peter. 'Jack asked me to call it. He has something very interesting to show us. I can't think why he's not here. It's past ten, and he said he'd be early.'

'I bet it's that awful sister of his who's stopping him coming,' said Pam.

'But how could she know about our meeting?' said Peter. 'Jack wouldn't tell her, I'm sure.'

'Here's Jack,' said Barbara, as more footsteps came down the path to the shed. Someone gave the door such a bang that they all jumped. Before Peter could call out 'Password' a voice shouted it loudly. 'WUFF-WUFF.'

7

'Enter!' cried Peter, sure it was Jack's voice. The door flew open – and there stood Susie, Jack's sister! She grinned round at them.

'Thanks for inviting me to your meeting,' she said, and shut the door behind her. She sat down on a box before anyone could stop her.

'Susie! How dare you!' shouted Peter and Janet together. Peter threw the door open. 'Go away!' he said. 'You know you've no right here. You don't belong to the Secret Seven.'

'Well, you'd better *let* me belong then,' said Susie. 'Because my mother says that the present Jack had from our Uncle Bob is to be shared between us! And as he's bringing it here to show you today, *I've* come to share it too.'

Someone else came down the path, carrying something over his shoulder – something long and straight. There was a loud knock on the door, and the password was said very clearly.

'Wuff-wuff,' said Jack's voice. It was exactly like

Susie's, so no wonder everyone had thought she was Jack!

'Enter!' called Peter. Jack came in, carrying his load carefully. He glared angrily at Susie.

'How did she know our password, Jack?' asked Peter, sternly. 'Did you tell her?'

'No, he didn't. I just hid in a bush outside and listened,' said Susie. 'You needn't glare at me like that, Jack. Mother said I could share that present, you know she did.'

'Can't we turn her out?' said Pam, who didn't like Susie at all. 'She always tries to spoil everything!'

'You just *try* to turn me out!' said Susie, fiercely. 'I don't want to come to your silly old meetings – but I tell you, I'm going to share Jack's present as much as any of *you* are.'

Peter looked at her in despair. What could you do with a girl like Susie? If they tried to turn her out she would probably shout and yell, and bring his mother down to see what was the matter – and Mother might even *agree* that Susie should stay and hear what Jack said about his present.

'Tomorrow Binkie, my friend, is coming to stay with me,' said Susie. 'And I've said *she* can share the present too – my half of it, I mean.'

'*Binkie* – that awful little rabbit-face?' said George, in horror. 'That silly giggler – that . . .'

Everyone groaned. Susie alone was bad enough, but when she and Binkie were together the two girls were impossible.

'Well – what are you going to do?' asked Susie. 'All rush on me together and throw me out? Or let me stay here at the meeting?'

Peter made up his mind quickly. On NO account could Susie attend one of the Secret Seven meetings. On the other hand they couldn't throw her out. She would make such a fuss! Very well then – he must declare the meeting ended, and say that there would be *no* proper meeting, but just a talk about Jack's present, whatever it was.

'I declare this Secret Seven meeting ended,' he said, in a loud voice. 'We will all go indoors and see Jack's present in our playroom. I will NOT have strangers present at our secret meetings.' He got up, and all the others stood too – except Susie.

'All right, all right – you win,' she said. 'Your mother would be cross with me, I know, if I go indoors with you. She'll think I've interfered. But just you listen for a minute, and hear *my* side of the question!'

CHAPTER THREE

JACK'S PRESENT

BUT BEFORE Susie could go on, footsteps pattered up to the shed-door, and someone scraped at the bottom. 'Password!' shouted Peter, and a doggy voice answered at once, 'WUFF-WUFF-WUFF!'

'Enter, Scamper,' said Peter. 'But you said too many wuffs! Clever dog, to remember the password!'

That made them all laugh, even Susie. Scamper trotted in and licked everyone in delight. Then he lay down at Peter's feet, panting. 'You're late, Scamper,' said Peter. 'But it doesn't matter because I've declared the meeting ended. Susie, if you've anything to say, say it, and go.'

'All right,' said Susie. 'That thing Jack has brought is a present from our Uncle Bob, who was once a sailor. It's a telescope – and a really fine one, too!'

'*A telescope!*' said everyone, excited. Yes – now they could see that it was. Jack began to take off the wrappings sulkily, as Susie went on talking.

'Well, Jack's idea was to bring it down here and give it to the Secret Seven,' said Susie. 'But Mother said Uncle Bob meant *me* to share it – and I didn't see why you Secret Seven should have it all. I knew I'd never see it once it was installed in this shed. So I argued with Jack . . .'

'Shouted the place down, you mean!' said poor Jack.

'And Mother heard, and she came, and she said Jack *was* to share the telescope with me, though she was pleased that the Secret Seven could look through it too. And Jack said he didn't care what Mother said, he wasn't going to let me share any of it – so I shot off by myself and came to the meeting to tell you all this.'

'And left me behind with Mother in a real rage,' said Jack. 'I'm so sorry, everyone. I meant to leave the telescope here in the shed, so that we could all use it, and look at all sorts of things in the distance – the different cars going along the hillside road – the castle on the hill – the herons on the old pond – it would have been such fun.'

'Yes – fun for *you* – but not for me!' said Susie. 'And what about Binkie? *You* want to share the telescope with Peter and Janet and the rest, don't you – well, I want to share it with Binkie!'

'I shouldn't think Binkie knows what a telescope *is*!' said Jack. 'Her head's full of wool, not brains! *She* won't want to use a telescope.'

'Now listen,' said Peter, making up his mind quickly. 'You'll *have* to share with Susie, Jack, if your mother says so. But why shouldn't we keep it down here in the shed, so that *any* of us can use it at any time? Not at a special meeting or anything like that.'

'We'd have to keep the shed locked, then,' said Jack. 'This telescope is quite valuable, Uncle said. But that means that Susie will have to know where the key is!'

'Well – as long as she doesn't try to come to any of our meetings again and spoil them as she has spoilt today's, I don't see why she shouldn't know where the key is,' said Peter. 'We've got to be fair about this, Jack. I bet *my* mother would say I'd got to share with Janet if someone gave me something like this telescope. Let's be fair.'

'All right,' said Jack gloomily. '*Be* fair. But don't blame *me* if Susie and Binkie spy on us and find out all our secrets and passwords and everything.'

'Let's have something to eat and drink,' said Janet. 'We'll all feel better then. You'd better have some too, Susie. Being cross always makes people hungry.'

'Well, I'm *not* hungry,' said Susie, getting up. 'But thank you all the same Janet. I know when I'm not wanted. I only came to say I'm *going* to share the telescope.'

'Wait a bit,' said Colin, seeing that Susie was near tears, for all her boldness. 'Before you go we'd better arrange where the key is to be hidden. Then you'll know where to look for it.'

'Tell Jack, and *he* can tell me,' said Susie, stalking out of the door. 'Goodbye, stuck-ups! Wait till I tell Binkie about this!'

She slammed the door so hard that Scamper jumped and began to bark. Jack looked round at the others, feeling ashamed of his sister.

'Susie's got such a temper,' he said. 'I'm so sorry about this.'

'Let's not talk about Susie,' said Janet. 'She didn't go off because she didn't want to share our food – she went because she was afraid she was going to cry. And I can just imagine how awful she'd feel if she did – in front of all of us!'

So nobody said another word about Susie, but tucked into currant buns and macaroons and hot cocoa. Scamper had his share, and thoroughly enjoyed himself. He went to sniff all round the big, strange-looking parcel that Jack had brought into the shed.

'No one seems interested in my telescope except Scamper,' said Jack, in a forlorn voice. 'And I was so very excited about it.'

Peter clapped him on the shoulder. 'So are we! Come on – let's see this wonderful present!'

CHAPTER FOUR

THE WONDERFUL TELESCOPE

THE WRAPPINGS were soon off – and the Seven crowded round as Jack put the big telescope together, and showed them how the long tube could be stretched out even longer.

'You've no idea how far the telescope's eye can see,' he said. 'When I looked through it this morning before I came, I could see the scarecrow in the field half a mile from our house – and what is more I could see a sparrow or some bird sitting on his hat!'

'Do let's look through it,' said Janet, excited. 'Let's take it out into the garden, and train it on something far away.'

So they carried it out into the garden, and set it on its little stand on the broad top of the low garden

wall. Jack was very clever at adjusting the lens so that it focused properly, and made everything as clear as could be.

'Now that's exactly right,' said Jack, looking through the telescope. 'I've trained it on that little cottage over on the slope there. Before you look through the telescope tell me what you can see with your bare eyes.'

'Well – the cottage, of course,' said Pam. 'And something in the garden, I can't see what.'

'And somebody on the path. That's about all,' said Barbara.

'Right. Well, look through the telescope and you'll see a whole lot more!' said Jack. 'You first, Peter – you're our leader.'

So Peter looked through the long telescope, and immediately gave a loud cry. 'Jack! It's marvellous! I can see Mrs Haddon as if she was just over our wall – and I can even see the jug she is carrying. And that's a pram in the garden – and I can see the baby's teddy bear sitting up at the end of it! And—'

'Let *me* have a turn,' said Janet, itching to have a look. 'Goodness! I can see something sticking out of the chimney! It must be a chimney sweep's brush. Yes, it is! And there's a cat sitting just inside the window! Oh Jack – it's as if I've magic eyes that can see for miles! Oh, aren't you lucky to have a telescope like this? What fun we'll have!'

Jack was very pleased at the excitement his telescope caused, as one after another the Secret Seven peered through it. 'We can have great fun with it,' he said, proudly. 'We can watch the birds and see everything they do. We can examine every aeroplane that comes overhead. We can—'

'Children! Whatever *are* you doing standing still out in the cold for so long?' suddenly cried a voice. 'You'll get colds, all of you! What's that you've got?'

'It's a telescope, Mother,' called Janet. 'It belongs to Jack. He's sharing it with us.'

'How lovely! But do you know how late it's getting?' called her mother.

'Well, we'll put the telescope away now,' said Jack. 'I'm supposed to get home to an early lunch. Come on – help me with it, Colin.'

Soon the telescope was safely in the shed, wrapped up very carefully.

'It's very good of you to share it with us,' said Peter, 'and to say we can all use it when we like. But I think we'd better say that I or Janet must be told when anyone comes to borrow it – we'll be *responsible* for it, see? Is that understood, everyone?'

'Oh yes! We'll come and tell you when we want to look through it,' said George, and the others agreed. 'But suppose you're out? We'd better know where the key of the shed is to be kept, Peter.'

'Oh – of course,' said Peter. 'Let's think now – somewhere fairly easy to get – but yet well hidden. What about under this flat stone here, just by the shed? Scamper, you're the only one not allowed to touch the stone or the key. Understand?'

'Wuff,' said Scamper solemnly and wagged his tail. He watched while Peter carefully slid the key under the stone.

'I'll have to tell Susie where it is,' said Jack, in rather a small voice.

'I know. We promised that,' said Peter. 'She will *have* to go into our shed, but we'll be careful not to leave any Secret Seven secrets about! Tell her where the key is – and say she MUST put it back under the stone if she ever uses it.'

'Right,' said Jack. 'Er – what about a new password, Peter? Susie knows our last one.'

'Goodness, yes. I'd forgotten that,' said Peter. 'Well, I think it's quite obvious what we'll have! The next password, members, is – TELESCOPE!'

Then off they all went, and Peter and Janet carried everything carefully back to the house. Scamper followed them, wagging his tail. 'Wuff-wuff!' he said, and Peter laughed. 'No – that's our *old* password, Scamper. You'll have to remember the *new* one!'

CHAPTER FIVE

THROUGH THE TELESCOPE

THE TELESCOPE was a great success. The Secret Seven found it a most fascinating pastime to peer through it at all kinds of things, and there was much coming and going at the meeting-shed.

'I'm writing an essay on gulls in wintertime,' said George, arriving one dinner hour, complete with sandwiches to eat. 'I thought I'd set up the telescope and watch the gulls on your father's fields, Peter – there are always so many there, at this time of year.'

So there sat George, solemnly chewing ham sandwiches, and peering through the telescope at the excited gulls foraging in a newly ploughed field. No wonder he had ten out of ten for his essay!

Colin wanted to see the big jet-liners that flew steadily on their way overhead. 'I could almost see what the people were having for dinner,' he told an astonished Janet. But she wasn't interested in planes – she loved to swing the telescope round on its stand, and watch the people walking or riding on the distant road.

'It's almost as if they were in the garden,' she said. 'Peter, I saw old Mrs King riding on her tricycle, and I counted the onions in her net-bag – twelve she had. And I saw that horrid little Harry Jones ride by the greengrocer's cart and quickly take an orange off it as he went.'

'You'll turn into a peeping Tom if you don't look out,' said Peter. 'I bet young Harry would be horrified if he knew you were watching him across dozens of fields!'

The telescope was used at night too, and the Seven marvelled at the way in which it brought the moon so close to them. They had to take the telescope indoors for that, because Peter's mother said it was too cold to stay outside with it.

Susie came to use it too, of course, with her friend Binkie, who was just as giggly as ever. They found the key and went into the shed. They took the telescope into the garden and rested it on the wall. Peter saw them there, and went out to them.

'Oooh, run, Susie – here's Peter!' giggled Binkie, pretending to be scared. 'Oh, don't eat us, will you, Peter! Oooh, I'm frightened of you.'

'I only came to see that you knew how to use the telescope,' said Peter, coldly. 'I thought Susie might want help.'

Susie was busy looking through the telescope. She had it trained on a house some way off – then she swung it to another house. 'There's Mr Roneo painting his greenhouse,' she said. 'The ladder's awfully wobbly. And now I can see Miss Fellows cleaning her window from inside. Now I'm looking at the roof of that big old house – I can see it sticking up above the trees. There's a skylight set in the roof – it's being opened – someone's climbing out! Oh! OH! OH!'

Her sudden loud screaming made Peter jump in fright. 'What's the matter? What's happening?' he demanded. 'Let me see.' But Susie fended Peter off and kept her eye glued to the telescope. 'Someone else has climbed out on the roof now!' she cried. 'And he's chasing the first man. Oh, he's fallen off the roof! Peter, what shall we do? We'd better tell your mother, and get help.'

'Mother's out,' said Peter, worried. 'I'll rush off myself and see what I can do. There's a doctor who lives opposite that old house. I could get him if he's there. What a bit of luck you happened to look through the telescope just then!'

He tore off down the garden – but when he came to the gate, he heard a noise that made him pause. It was the sound of delighted giggling!

He stopped at once – and then strode back angrily.

'What are you laughing at, Binkie? Susie, *did* you really see a man fall off the roof – or not?'

'Well – he might *not* have fallen off,' said Susie. 'I'll look again.' She put her eye to the telescope and peered through it once more. 'I can still see him! He's got his foot caught in the roof gutter now – oh, Poor man, he's hanging upside-down by one foot. Now here comes the other man, he—'

'Idiot!' said Peter, angrily. 'All made up, of course! I might easily have gone off to that house and taken the doctor too, and hunted for an imaginary man down in the garden. I suppose you think that's funny?'

'Oh we do, we do!' said Susie, with tears of laughter in her eyes. 'It's *awfully* funny, Peter – you should just have seen your face of horror. This is a most wonderful telescope. I wonder what I'll see next. *You* have a turn, Binkie, and see if you can spot anything interesting too.'

'You can both clear off,' said Peter, and took firm hold of the telescope. 'If *this* is the kind of thing

29

you're going to use a telescope for, I shall lock it up. Go HOME, BOTH OF YOU!'

And dear me, he looked so fierce, and Scamper began to bark so loudly that Susie and Binkie actually obeyed him, and fled for their lives!

CHAPTER SIX

A FACE AT THE WINDOW!

IT WASN'T until Janet thought she would turn the tele-scope on to the big hill where the ruined old castle of Torling stood, that anything really exciting turned up. The castle wasn't much more than a few standing walls, and one great ruined tower in which jackdaws nested.

Janet liked the jackdaws. They sometimes flew down to the farm, and pecked about with the hens, talking all the time in their chattery voices.

'Chack-chack-chack!' they called to one another. Jack and Pam were with Janet the last time she had gone to watch the jackdaws in the fields, and Jack had made them laugh by saying that he kept wanting to say 'Yes, sir!' every time a jackdaw called 'Chack!'

'It sounds exactly as if they're yelling at me,' said Jack, 'just like our games teacher does at football!'

'Chack! Chack!' called a big jackdaw at once, cocking his head on one side and looking up at Jack. 'Chack! Chack!'

'There! He heard what I said,' said Jack, and they all laughed.

The jackdaws nested in the ruins of the old tower, but now that it was November their young ones were grown, and were flying with them. The little colony must have numbered at least a hundred. Janet could see them from her bedroom window, and had often wished the old tower was nearer the farm, so that she could watch the antics of the birds more closely.

And now I *can*! she thought. We've got that lovely telescope that brings everything so near! Why didn't I think of watching the jackdaws before!

She went to fetch it, first telling Peter in case he wanted it himself. 'It's really too cold to sit out in the open air with it today,' he said, as he took the key out from under the stone. 'Better take the telescope indoors, Janet. I'll carry it in for you. We could put it up in the boxroom at the top of the house – you'd be out of the way then – and the big window there looks right up the hill to the castle.'

Soon Janet was sitting in the boxroom, surrounded by all kinds of junk, her eye glued to the bottom end of the telescope tube. She had trained it carefully on to the top of the faraway hill, where the jackdaws circled round the tower, a hundred small black dots in the far distance.

But now, seen through the telescope they became birds, not dots – birds with outspread wings, circling and rising and falling in the misty November day. They played tricks on one another, chased each other, pretended to tumble and then swept away crying 'chack-chack-chack' as if they were laughing. Janet laughed too.

And then she suddenly stiffened on her chair. She was looking at one of the old windows at the top of

the tower, through which some of the jackdaws had been flying – but now there were no jackdaws there; they had flown away as if suddenly scared, when something appeared in the window-opening, peeping cautiously over the stone window-ledge.

What is it? thought Janet. It's not a bird. Surely it can't be a cat? No – it isn't – my goodness me, it's a *head* – a man's head with a hat on – no, a cap. What in the world is he doing?

The head remained at the window for a few minutes, and then disappeared. Janet knew that there were dangerous, broken steps at one side of the tower, leading almost to the top and she guessed that whoever it was who was there would now be climbing down. She trained the telescope downwards – and caught sight of something moving past one of the lower windows. The man was half-way down!

'Look at that!' she said out loud, astonished. 'Someone's hiding in that old tower! Whatever for? It's ruined and tumble-down and deserted – and dangerous too, because it's gradually subsiding! I must tell Peter!'

She yelled for him and he came up to the boxroom. Janet told him what she had seen, and he too looked through the telescope at the old castle. But he could see nothing moving there, except the jackdaws, who were now once more settling here and there on the castle walls.

'Whoever it was has gone into hiding down below,' said Janet, beginning to feel excited. 'So the jackdaws aren't frightened any longer. Who can it be, Peter?'

'Can't imagine!' said her brother, puzzled. 'Nobody ever goes there in the winter – and anyway, it's supposed to be dangerous now. Some stones fell down this spring, you know – right off the top of the tower! Are you quite *sure* you saw a face at the window? Which window was it?'

Janet told him, and Peter gazed at it through the telescope, moving it downwards to other openings. He gave a sudden exclamation.

'Yes! There *is* someone there! I saw something moving down below – on the ground floor. I'm sure someone passed quickly across the doorway, just inside! No wonder the jackdaws keep flying up in fright!'

'We must tell the Secret Seven,' said Janet, excited. 'You never know, Peter – this might be something mysterious, something that . . .'

Peter laughed. 'It's probably just some tramp looking for shelter! Still, we'll tell the others and see what *they* think!'

CHAPTER SEVEN

SUSIE IS VERY ANNOYING

NEXT DAY, when Peter walked home with Jack and George after school, he told them what he and Janet had seen through the telescope. 'Janet saw a face – the head of a man wearing a cap,' he said. 'And I distinctly saw someone moving behind the great doorway of the castle. I think there's a man hiding up there.'

'Well, if he were hiding, surely he wouldn't give himself away by peering through windows and walking across open doorways!' objected Jack. 'I expect it was just a chance visitor.'

'Look, Jack – anyone hiding up there would never, never imagine that anybody could *possibly* spot him in the castle, far away from everywhere, at the top of that hill!' said Peter. 'It was only because we were using your powerful telescope that that man was seen! He could never be spotted with the naked eye.'

'Yes – you're right there,' said George. 'I didn't think of that. The castle is so lonely and deserted on the top of that steep hill that anyone might judge it safe to hide there in the wintertime. But it must be so cold! Where does he sleep, do you think?'

'Down in the old dungeons?' suggested Peter, with a shiver. 'Have you ever seen them? You go down about a hundred steps into a cold, dark, echoing place – rather like a most *enormous* cellar! Hundreds of years ago prisoners were kept down there.'

'How horrible people must have been in those days!' said George. 'I couldn't even keep a dog or cat down in a cellar!'

'What about us going up to the old castle and having a snoop round?' said Jack. 'I've never been there.'

'Well, it's rather dangerous now, my dad says,' said George. 'But the dangerous places have warning notices up, so I dare say we'd be all right. After all, we're pretty sensible, or Peter wouldn't allow us to belong to the Secret Seven!'

That made the others laugh. 'Quite right,' said Peter. 'No idiots allowed in the S.S. Club! Well, what about it – *shall* we go up to the castle? We could bike or walk, whichever you like.'

'Bike,' said Jack. 'It's true we'll have to walk up most of the castle hill, it's so steep – but it will be fun to coast down.'

'Right. Saturday morning, then,' said Peter. 'We'll ask Colin if he'd like to come, but not the girls – the hill would be a bit steep for them.'

But the three girls had quite other ideas about that. 'Too steep indeed!' snorted Janet, when Peter told her what he and the other boys had planned. 'I bet I could ride right up that hill and get to the top before you did! We're *all* coming, see? Pam and Barbara, too. This is a Secret Seven thing, and we'll all be in it. Anyway, *I* discovered there was someone hiding in the castle, not you!'

'All right, all right, all *right*,' said Peter, backing away. 'Don't bite my nose off. I'll ring up Jack and tell him it's to be a Secret Seven outing. We'll all wear our badges.'

So he rang up Jack, and told him that Janet insisted on the three girls coming.

'What a nuisance!' said Jack. 'It's quite a way to the castle – and we'll have to bike slowly or the girls won't keep up with us.'

'What's this you're phoning about?' said Susie, suddenly appearing at the door of the room in which Jack was phoning. 'Are you going on a spree or something? I'd like to come too. It would be a treat for Binkie.'

'Well, you're *not* coming!' said Jack. 'It's a Secret Seven outing. And do shut up a minute. Can't you see I'm phoning?' He turned back to the telephone. 'Sorry, Peter. Susie came barging in just then. She said *she* wanted to come too, with Binkie!'

'What a truly horrible idea!' said Peter into the phone. 'They can't, of course. I won't have them.'

'Have you spotted that man again, hiding in the castle?' asked Jack, thinking that Susie had gone out of the room.

'Don't talk about that on the phone,' said Peter, quite cross. 'Anyone might hear! It's *our* secret!'

'Sorry,' said Jack, humbly. 'All right, then – we all of us meet at a quarter to ten, Saturday morning, outside your front gate. Is Scamper coming?'

'No. Too long a run for him,' said Peter. 'Goodbye for now!'

Susie pounced on Jack as soon as he had finished. She had been hiding behind an armchair, listening! Jack glared at her in rage.

'You've been *listening*! Well, a fat lot of good it will do you!' And he stalked out of the room.

'Who's hiding in the old castle? And why are they there, do you think?' asked Susie, following Jack out of the room. 'Go on – tell me. How do you *know* anyone's there? It's too far to see people in the castle. I don't believe it!'

'You forget that we have a telescope, Miss Clever!' said Jack, coldly, and ran up the stairs. Susie made a rude face behind his back.

'Well, *we're* coming too, Binkie and I,' she said. 'We'll be the Secret Nine, instead of the Secret Seven! So there!'

CHAPTER EIGHT

UP AT THE CASTLE

JACK KNEW perfectly well that Susie would keep her word, and that she and Binkie would follow the Seven on their journey to the old castle. He kicked himself for not having made certain that his annoying sister was out of the room before he finished phoning. He would remember to search thoroughly in future.

With a sigh he went to see Peter, not daring to telephone him again, in case Susie was about. He told him of Susie's threat.

'Well – fancy letting out what our plans were, with *Susie* in the room!' said Peter, in disgust. 'You really *are* a fool! Never mind. We'll simply start half an hour later – but for goodness' *sake* don't let her guess that!'

So, at quarter past ten on Saturday morning, the Secret Seven assembled outside Peter's front gate. All of them had their bicycles with them, and in the baskets were bottles of lemonade, and biscuits. This was Janet's idea, and everyone thought it a very good one.

Jack was the last to arrive, and he pedalled up in a hurry. 'Sorry I'm late,' he said. 'I had to make sure that Susie and Binkie weren't lying in wait somewhere, meaning to come with me!'

'Where are they?' demanded Peter.

'I don't know. But their bikes are still in the shed, so we're safe,' said Jack, thankfully. 'I asked Mother where they were, and she said she heard them talking about going shopping – so *that's* all right!'

'All the same – we'll keep a lookout till we're safely on the way,' said Peter. 'I will *not* have those two messing up our plans.'

They saw no sign whatever of Susie or Binkie and soon forgot about them. After all, if their bikes were in the shed, they couldn't go far!

When they came to the steep road that wound up round the castle hill, they panted and puffed – and one by one leapt off to walk. It really was *too* steep to ride up. The road did not go to the castle, but passed by it some way off. A footpath over a stile led to the old ruin, and when they came to this the Seven piled their bicycles on top of one another in the hedge, and were soon over the stile. They carried their lemonade and biscuits with them, planning to eat and drink in the shelter of the castle.

It was still some way off up the hill. They all kept a sharp lookout for signs of anyone looking out of the windows, but could see nothing at all.

The jackdaws circled overhead all the time, calling loudly, disturbed at seeing so many children. 'Chack, chack!' they called. 'Chack, chack!'

And Jack answered at once. 'Glad you know me! How are you all?'

'Idiot!' said Peter, laughing. 'Wow – what an enormous number there are! Now, what shall we do first?

Look round the old place – go down into the dungeons and snoop around? Eat our biscuits?'

'Let's go inside and eat there,' said Barbara. 'The wind's very strong out here, and I'm cold. I'm hungry, too. We can snoop round afterwards.'

So they all trooped up the broken steps, and in at the great entrance to the castle, where once enormous gates had hung. They stopped in the vast hall inside, and stared in surprise. It was piled high at one side with twigs of all kinds and sizes!

'Who put those here?' said Jack, puzzled. 'Oh, of course – the jackdaws! They nest in the tower chimney, and these twigs must have fallen down from their nests for years and years!'

They looked up the tower. They could see the sky through a square hole at the top where smoke once rose from the enormous stone fireplace far below, in the hall. This was almost completely hidden by the fallen twigs, which had spread out on to the hall floor as well. They cracked loudly as the children trod on them.

A big wooden notice, with DANGER painted on it, was placed further down the hall, in a carved stone doorway. The children peered through it, and saw a big room, with one wall crumbling dangerously. It looked as if it might fall at any time.

'We can't go in *there*,' said Peter, at once. 'I shouldn't think anyone would hide in *that* room – I imagine it would be a pretty dangerous hiding-place!'

'Sh!' said Janet, in a low voice. 'Don't talk about hiding-places – if anyone *is* hiding here, they'll hear you.'

'You're right,' said Peter. 'Let's go further down the hall – we'll find plenty more old rooms, I expect, all crumbling away! Come on – and look out for any signs of people hiding!' he added, in a whisper. 'Follow me!'

CHAPTER NINE

AN EXCITING TIME!

IT WASN'T until they came to what seemed to be a dark kitchen-like place, with a huge stone sink in one corner, that they found anything at all exciting. Jack suddenly stopped and pointed.

The others looked, and saw what appeared to have been a fire, made of sticks, half-burnt through. Pam gave a little cry as she bent over them.

'Hey – the sticks are still warm! It's not long since this fire was lit!'

'Sh!' said everyone, looking over their shoulders, feeling that whoever had lit that fire might still be about.

Peter felt the twigs. Yes, they were certainly still warm – and what was more, it looked as if someone had stamped out the little fire in a hurry, for it was curiously flattened!

'Talk in loud voices about ordinary things,' commanded Peter, in a whisper. 'And keep your eyes open.'

They followed Peter up some steps to a stone bench in a crumbling recess in the wall. A newspaper had been left there, and they pounced on it.

'What date is it? It might tell us whether anyone has been here recently,' said Colin. He shook it open.

'No – no use,' he said. 'Look – it's dated sixteenth September – ages ago!'

'Left by some visitor, probably – maybe trippers were still visiting the castle then,' said Peter. 'Come on – let's have another look round.'

To their great disappointment they could find nothing of any use at all. A few cigarette ends – one or two dead matches – a paper bag that had once held sweets. 'No – I can't say that these are any help,' said Peter.

'I vote we sit down and have our biscuits,' said George, at last, tired of hunting in every corner. 'I'm filthy dirty – just look at my hands!'

'Hey – do you suppose these steps go down to the dungeons?' called Barbara. Everyone turned to see where she was. She stood below a big hand-printed notice. It said: 'THE DUNGEONS. UNSAFE. DESCENT FORBIDDEN.'

'Yes. Look at the notice, idiot,' said Peter. 'Well – we don't go down those steps, that's certain! I don't particularly want an old wall to fall on top of me!'

'Let's have our biscuits sitting on the old stone bench here,' said Jack. 'It will just about take us all. What a castle! The things that must have happened here!'

They all sat down, crowding on to the uneven old seat. It felt very cold and hard! Soon they were munching their biscuits, and drinking their lemonade out of the little bottles.

'Do you really think anyone's here besides us – hiding somewhere?' said Pam, in a whisper.

'Quite likely,' answered Peter, also in a whisper. 'Probably down in the dungeons! Nobody in their senses would go down there, with that danger notice up!'

'I don't like to think of someone hiding down in that horrible dark dungeon,' said Barbara, a picture of a dreadful damp, smelly, black place coming into her mind. 'I do hope to goodness we don't hear any noises coming from there.'

'Don't be a silly fool,' said George. 'Nobody's down there – why should—'

He stopped very suddenly, as a curious noise suddenly came to his ears. Everyone heard it, and stiffened in fright.

It sounded a little like a very unhappy owl. 'Ooooo!' it wailed. 'Ooo-oo-OOOOOOO!'

Pam clutched Barbara and made her jump. 'What is it? Did you hear?'

'Shut up,' said Peter, sharply. 'Listen, everyone. Someone's down in those dungeons.'

AN EXCITING TIME!

'Oooh-ah-oooh-eeeee!' wailed the voice.

Pam gave such a shriek that everyone leapt to their feet. She tumbled down from the seat and ran howling down the stone passage to the hall.

Jack went after her, and the others were just collecting their bags and bottles when another noise made them jump. It, too, came from the dungeons.

'Bang! Bang-bang! Bang!'

'Quick – run!' shouted Peter, clutching Janet, and pushing her in front of him. 'Back to our bikes!'

'Is that someone shooting?' asked Barbara, fearfully, as they ran, hearing a few more 'bangs' coming from the dungeons.

'Goodness knows!' said Peter. 'Gosh, look how scared the jackdaws are now – and what a row they are making! Whatever can be going on in that castle?'

CHAPTER TEN

ANOTHER MEETING

WHEN THEY had reached their bicycles safely, they paused to put their bags and bottles into the baskets. Peter was beginning to feel a bit ashamed of their hurried flight.

'Do you think we boys ought to go back and find out what those bangs were?' he said. 'I mean – I don't *think* they were gun-shots, you know – they weren't loud enough.'

'You go if you want to. *I'm* not rushing into danger,' said Colin. 'Something's certainly going on there. Tell the police if you like – and leave *them* to deal with it. What with that half-warm, stamped-out fire of twigs – and those howls and bangs – it's enough to scare grown-ups, let alone *us*!'

ANOTHER MEETING

'Let's have a meeting about it!' said George. 'We ought to decide what we're going to do. We *know* there's somebody there – so why is he hiding? And what's he doing down in the dungeons, popping away like that? Is he trying to scare us off? Has he something to hide?'

'Let's have a meeting as soon as we get back,' said Janet.

'I can't. I've a music lesson at quarter past twelve,' said Pam. 'Please, *please* don't have a meeting without me.'

'Well, three o'clock this afternoon, then,' said Peter. 'And mind you remember the password – telescope – and wear your badges.'

'*I* can't come then,' said Jack, 'and neither can George. We've got football practice. Make it tomorrow evening.'

'All right. Tomorrow evening then – six o'clock – and be punctual,' said Peter. 'And if I've got time I'll take a look at that castle through the telescope this afternoon. There really *is* something going on there!'

They rode home rather gloomily, all the boys now wishing they had gone into the dungeons – or at least peeped down – to see what was going on. 'Still, we hadn't any torches,' said Peter. 'We couldn't have seen a thing. It sounded very much like owls, didn't it, but it couldn't have been. Owls hoot but they don't make bang-bang noises!'

Jack rode home, hoping that Susie and Binkie were out still and wouldn't ask him questions about his morning. He peeped into the shed and saw that the girls' bikes were still there. Good! They must still be out doing their Saturday shopping!

As soon as Peter was home, he fetched the telescope from the shed, while a delighted Scamper danced round him. The spaniel had not been at all pleased at being left behind that morning, and had lain by the fire, sulking – but now he was so glad to see Peter and Janet again that he could hardly keep still!

Peter took the telescope to the boxroom and set it up. Scamper sniffed at the bottom end with much interest.

'You look up it with your eye, not your *nose*,' said Peter. He set his right eye to the telescope, and trained it on the castle – goodness, was that someone standing in the great doorway?

But before he could see properly, Scamper jumped up to lick him – and over went the telescope! 'Idiot!' said Peter, crossly, and hurriedly picked it up. It seemed all right. He set it up again and peered through it excitedly.

But now the doorway was empty. No one stood there. Peter felt really vexed. 'Couldn't you have waited a bit to lick me?' he said to Scamper. 'Oh goodness – now there's *Mother* calling me – and by the time I get back to the boxroom, it'll be too late to spot whoever it was!'

His mother kept him busy for the rest of the morning, and in the afternoon he had to do his homework.

He longed to go up and look through the telescope. So did Janet.

There was nothing interesting to be seen when at last they managed to peer through it. In disappointment they took it down to the shed again, and locked it there as usual.

'Cheer up, Peter,' said Janet. 'We're having a meeting tomorrow night, and I've a box of toffees! It will be fun to talk about our morning at the castle.'

On Sunday evening everyone arrived quite punctually, and the password was rattled out five times. 'Telescope!' As George said, it would be easier to remember *that* password than forget it!

They settled down in the warm shed, all seven of them. Peter glanced round to see if they were wearing their badges. Yes – everyone had the S.S. on their coats. Janet handed round the toffees, and they began to talk about the previous morning.

'Someone's hiding at the castle, for *some* reason, that's certain,' began Peter. 'And that someone doesn't want anyone else to know he's there – and scared us away. I feel silly now – I'm sure the man who's hiding there knew we were kids and would run for our lives if he made scary noises!'

'Yes. I've been thinking that too,' said Jack.

'Oh, but they sounded so *awful*,' said Pam, and she gave a little shudder. 'I wouldn't go there again if you gave me a thousand pounds.'

'Well, we're not offering you anything like that,' said Peter. 'So stop shuddering, and talk sense. I think now that we were rather cowardly.'

'But those *bangs*!' said Barbara. 'They sounded so loud and frightening. And those moans and howls!'

'Now let's be sensible,' said Peter. 'I don't suppose—'

And then he stopped very suddenly indeed, for from outside the shed came two or three mournful yowls exactly like those the Seven had heard yesterday morning! 'Ooo-oo-OOOO!'

Everyone jumped violently, and Scamper barked and ran to the door, scratching it angrily. There was a dead silence in the shed, except for Scamper. The moaning suddenly stopped.

Then the bangs began! Pop! Pop-pop! POP!

'I'm scared,' whispered Pam, and clutched at Barbara, making her jump.

'Ooo-ooo! Pop-bang-pop!'

Then came a most familiar sound – a giggle, hastily stopped midway. Jack and Peter gave cries of fury and rushed to the door.

'SUSIE! BINKIE! YOU BEASTS!'

The door was flung open so suddenly that the two giggling girls outside were taken by surprise. Jack leapt out and caught Susie. Binkie ran, but came back to help Susie and was caught too. They were both dragged into the shed and set down with a bump on two boxes.

'And now will you just tell us the *meaning* of all this!' said Peter, so angry that he could hardly get the words out of his mouth.

CHAPTER ELEVEN

SUSIE'S TALE

'I SHAN'T say a word if you shout at me,' said Susie. 'And Binkie and I will yell the place down if you're unkind to us.'

'Unkind! UNKIND! Well, what about you and Binkie!' cried Janet. 'Interfering in all our plans! It was *you* down in that dungeon, wasn't it – yowling and – and – well, what *were* you doing to make those bangs?'

'They weren't bangs – they were loud pops,' said Susie, with a sudden giggle. 'The same as we made down in that dungeon. Look – I'll show you!' The two girls looked highly pleased with themselves.

And to the great disgust of the Secret Seven she took a small bundle of coloured rubber out of her pocket and blew hard into it. It swelled up into a truly colossal balloon! Susie held it away from her and Binkie promptly jabbed it with a large pin. POP!

'*That's* what scared you away – balloons popping – and yowls!' said Binkie, giving them a wicked grin, and putting the big pin back under her coat lapel. 'Did our hoots and yowls sound awful coming up those old stone steps?'

'You'd no right to go down into those dungeons,' said Peter, severely. 'Didn't you see the notice? Don't tell me *you* put that notice there!'

'No, we didn't. But it wasn't there when I went up to see the castle with some friends in the summer,' said Binkie, 'so I guessed it couldn't be *very* danger-ous to go down! It was only printed by hand too – not properly, like the other notices.'

'So it was,' said Jack, remembering. 'Hey – do you suppose that whoever is hiding there wrote out that notice himself, to stop people prying in the dungeons?'

'And stop them finding something he had hidden there!' exclaimed George. 'It's just like Susie to disobey warnings.'

'*Did* you see anything hidden there?' said Peter. 'Tell us at once.'

'Yes, we did,' said Susie. 'But unless you ask me politely, I shan't tell you anything.'

Peter glared at her. Exasperating, irritating girl! She grinned cheekily at him. 'Say "please, Susie",' she said.

And poor Peter had to do as he was told! He just *had* to know what was down in the dungeons.

'Please, Susie,' he said, quite fiercely.

'Not like that. Really *politely*,' said Susie.

'SUSIE! I'll shake you to bits if you go on like this!' said Jack suddenly. 'I'm ashamed of you – talking to Peter like that. I'll – I'll . . .'

'All right, all right. I'll tell you what we saw,' said Susie, hastily, knowing quite well that her brother would certainly give her a really good shaking if she was cheeky much longer. 'Listen, all of you.'

Everyone listened intently as Susie told what had happened to her and Binkie yesterday morning. Binkie sat beside her, nodding her head every now and then as Susie related her story.

'Well,' began Susie, 'we knew you were all going up there, of course, and we knew you thought there was someone hiding in the castle, because we heard what Jack said on the phone. So we thought we'd go too, and get there *before* you, so that we could play a few tricks.'

'Yes – but how did you get there? Your bikes were in the shed. I saw them,' said Jack.

'Have you forgotten that there are such things as buses?' said Susie. 'We just caught the bus that goes up the hill and stops at the top. We hopped off and made our way over the fields to the castle – to the *back* of it, not the front, in case you came early.'

'*Buses!* Why didn't we think of that!' groaned Jack. 'So you were there a long time before us?'

'Oh yes – and when we came up to the back of the castle, very quietly, just in *case* anyone was there, we saw someone sitting on an old stone, painting the castle.'

'Painting a *picture* of it, she means,' put in Binkie, seeing that some of the Seven looked rather astonished. 'Goodness – she jumped like anything when we came up behind her, because she hadn't heard us coming over the grass.'

'Did you talk to her?' asked Peter. '*We* thought it was a man there, not a woman. The person I saw through the telescope seemed to have a man's cap on.'

'Oh, this woman had no cap – but she wears her hair sort of piled up on top of her head. I suppose it looked like a cap, in the distance,' said Susie, who was now enjoying herself thoroughly. 'Well—'

Scamper suddenly growled and ran to the door. 'Someone's coming!' said Peter. 'Who is it?'

There was a knock at the door, and then came his mother's cheerful voice. 'I won't come in, I know you're talking secrets – but I'm leaving a plate of jam-tarts out here. Seven – is that right?'

'No, nine – ten, counting Scamper!' called Susie, cheekily, before anyone else could say a word. 'It's a Secret *Nine* Meeting tonight!'

'Well, one of you must come and fetch two more then,' she replied, and off she went back to the house.

'Secret *Nine* indeed!' said Janet, very cross. She frowned angrily at Susie. 'You certainly *won't* get any tarts!'

'Right. We'll say goodbye and go home then,' said Susie. 'Come on, Binkie!' And the two of them got up and went to the door!

CHAPTER TWELVE

SUSIE HAS PLENTY TO SAY!

PETER GROANED. He knew when he was beaten! 'All right – you win!' he said. 'Come back and sit down. Colin, go and get three more jam-tarts – old Scamper can have one then.'

Colin departed, with Scamper at his heels. The rest of the Seven sat and looked at Susie in disgust. What a girl! She smiled cheekily all round. This certainly was Her Evening! Aha! She was teaching those stuck-up Seven a lesson!

Colin came back at once with the tarts, and they all began to eat them, Scamper too.

'Well, about this artist woman,' said Susie, with her mouth full. 'She said we'd better not go into the castle because it was dangerous, so we thanked her for her warning – but, of course, we meant to go without her seeing us!'

'You *would*!' said Jack.

'We stopped and talked a bit, just to see if she had anything interesting to say,' said Susie. 'But she hadn't, really. She just said she loved the old castle, and was painting it, hoping to sell the picture. She said she kept her paints and things inside, because nobody ever came in the winter, so they were quite safe.'

'This looks as if all our suspicions were silly,' said Peter, feeling rather small.

'She was awfully interested in us, too,' went on Susie. 'Wasn't she, Binkie?'

'Oh yes – she asked us a lot of questions – and she laughed like anything when Susie said Jack and the others were coming up to hunt a man hiding in the castle.'

'You told her *that*!' cried Peter, angrily. 'How dare you? You'd no right to give our plans away.'

'Well, they were silly plans, so it didn't really matter,' said Susie. 'She asked me how in the world you could see anyone in the castle from this farm – we told her you lived here, Peter – and she was *very* interested to hear about the telescope we keep down in this shed, and how easily we could see the castle with it.'

'SUSIE! You surely didn't give that away too – how *could* you? Now she'll know we're watching what's happening,' groaned Peter. 'Honestly, you must be a nitwit to jabber like that to a stranger.'

'And *you* must be a nitwit to think anything peculiar is going on up at the castle,' said Susie. 'Just a woman artist painting a picture! *No* one's hiding there. She said that she goes down to sleep in the village on the other side of the castle each night – and except for us, not a soul has been to the castle since she came. Ha ha – what about your mystery now?'

The Secret Seven felt very small indeed – and very angry. It had all been so exciting – and now Susie had interfered, and there was nothing left!

'Did you see anything at all in the dungeons?' asked Peter, after a pause.

'Only things that I suppose belonged to the artist,' said Susie. 'Let's see – what was there, Binkie?'

'Pictures,' said Binkie. 'Pictures without frames. Rather dark and ugly, *I* thought. I suppose the artist had painted them. They were all covered up, of course. We just peeped at them. There was a pile of rugs too, and some tins.'

'The artist said she'd take another day or two to finish the picture, and when it rained she went into the castle for shelter,' said Susie. 'That's how it was you saw her peeping out of that window, I expect. She has all her meals there too, except breakfast and supper. She just opens a tin.'

'Funny sort of life,' said George. 'Well – that's that! If only we'd gone behind the castle *we'd* have seen her too. We just went straight in at the front. You were watching out for us, I suppose, and shot down into the cellar to blow up your stupid balloons.'

'We nearly died of laughing when we heard you yelling with fright, and listened to you racing out of the castle,' said Binkie, and went off into one of her giggling fits.

'Oh do shut up,' said Jack, tired of both Binkie and Susie. 'Go home. Get out of our sight.'

'We thought we'd like to use the telescope, if you don't mind,' said Susie, putting on a most polite voice. 'The moon's rather good tonight.'

'No. This meeting is ending,' said Peter, firmly. 'Scoot, you two girls. I think your behaviour was *disgraceful.*'

'You sound like Miss Cummings, our teacher,' said Susie, in delight. 'Do say all that again!'

'Oh clear out!' said Peter, at the end of his patience. 'And don't *attempt* to do anything funny with our telescope tonight. I forbid you to!'

'But it doesn't belong to *you*,' said Susie, flaring up at once. 'It's half mine. I only *let* you use my half-share in it, I—'

'SUSIE! Be quiet, and come home with me,' said Jack, and he took his sister's arm very firmly indeed. 'I'm ashamed of you!'

He dragged her out of the shed, and Binkie followed. Peter heaved a sigh of relief.

'Thank goodness, we've got rid of them! *What* a pair! Well, let's hope that's the last we'll hear of them for some time!'

CHAPTER THIRTEEN

THE TELESCOPE AGAIN

SUSIE AND Binkie were angry with Jack for hauling them away. 'We wanted to look through the telescope again,' complained Susie.

'No, you didn't – you were just being annoying,' said Jack, fiercely.

'Let go of my arm,' said Susie. 'I want to walk by myself.'

'Well, just behave yourself then,' said Jack, quite relieved to let such a wriggler go. The two girls darted off at once, and Jack saw them racing up the road towards home. He heaved a sigh of relief. What COULD anyone do with a sister like Susie?

But Susie and Binkie didn't go home. No – Susie was quite determined to have her way and take out the telescope that night. She didn't really want to – it was just obstinacy. She had asked for it – had been refused – and that had made her determined to get her own way. Just like Susie!

So, instead of going round the corner and home, the two girls slipped into a gateway, waited till Jack had gone plodding past, and then raced back to Peter's again. They were puffing and panting so much that they hadn't enough breath left to giggle. But they were very thrilled to think they had outwitted poor Jack, who would be almost home by now. Ha! Ha!

In no time they were down at the shed. It was in darkness now, and well and truly locked. The girls found the key under the stone, and unlocked the wooden door.

They each had a torch, and it was not difficult to set up the telescope on the low garden wall as usual.

'We'll just have a quick look at the moon, so that we can say we saw it through the telescope,' said

Susie. 'And then we'll put it away. Won't the Secret Seven be wild to think we got our way after all!'

They were soon looking through the long tube of the big telescope. The moon was not at all obliging, and stayed behind clouds, so that the night was dark, instead of light.

'Swing the telescope round a bit and look at the old castle,' suggested Binkie. 'Then we can say we saw that too.'

So Susie trained the telescope on to the castle, far away on its steep hill. It was just a great dark shadow in the night, only visible because of the light from the half-hidden moon.

'There,' said Susie, 'now we can . . . oooh – hey – Binkie, there's a *light* in the castle!'

'In the *castle*! What do you mean? Let *me* see!' said Binkie, and glued her eye to the bottom of the telescope. 'Yes! There *is* a light. It's somewhere on the ground floor – is it shining out of the entrance?'

'I don't know. Might be one of the downstairs windows,' said Susie, pushing Binkie aside. 'Yes, there it is – quite clear! What does that mean, do you suppose? That woman said she never slept in the castle – she went down to her lodgings for tea and stayed there! It's a signal to someone, I should think. Yes – that must be it. Perhaps there *is* something going on, after all!'

'Goodness! Let's go and tell Peter then,' said Binkie, excited. 'Or shall we keep it to ourselves?'

'No – we'll tell Peter,' said Susie. 'He'll be *furious* to think we've discovered something else! Come on!' So off they went to find Peter and Janet. They were up in their playroom, doing jigsaws, and were really amazed to see Binkie and Susie again!

'Look here!' began Peter angrily, but Susie stopped him.

'We've got news!' she said. 'There's someone up at the castle, signalling with a light! We saw it! We looked through the telescope. Come and see.'

But Peter only laughed, and sat down to his jigsaw again. '*Another* of your silly jokes,' he said. 'I wonder you're not tired of them. If you think we're going to be taken in again, you're mistaken. Now, if you don't clear out and *keep* out, I'll call Mother. We've had enough of you both for tonight.'

'But Peter – we looked through the—' began Binkie, and was promptly pushed out of the room by Peter and Janet, and Susie was hustled off too. The playroom door banged, and the two girls heard the key being turned in the lock.

'All right! You'll be sorry!' shouted Susie. 'You'll be VERY sorry tomorrow that you didn't listen to us!'

And down the stairs they went, almost crying with rage. There *was* someone signalling in that castle, there *was*!

CHAPTER FOURTEEN

A HORRID SHOCK

NEXT MORNING Janet and Peter went down to their shed after breakfast to clear up the things left there the evening before.

'We've twenty minutes before we need to start for school,' said Peter, looking for the key under the stone. 'Hallo – the key's not here! What's happened to it? I know I put it there last night.'

'Susie must have taken it!' said Janet, frowning. 'Just to spite us. The little nuisance!'

They went to the shed-door to see if Susie had torn off the green letters S.S. that were always there. Good – they were still there – but as they turned away from the shed, Janet gave a cry of surprise.

'Peter! The key's in the *lock*! Susie forgot to hide it – the idiot! Anyone might break into the shed and take things if it isn't locked.'

They went in, feeling cross. Everything seemed all right – and then Janet frowned. Something was missing, surely? What was it?

'The *telescope*!' she cried suddenly. 'Peter – where's the telescope? It's gone!'

'Susie's taken it!' said Peter, so angry that he stammered over the words. 'Just because I said she wasn't to use it, and because we wouldn't believe her silly story last night about someone signalling in the castle! I'm going to telephone Jack.'

Jack was horrified when he heard Peter's news. He fetched Susie at once.

'You just go to the phone and tell Peter where you've hidden the telescope!' he said. 'It's not in the shed.'

'But we put it back safely,' said Susie, sounding so amazed that Jack felt she must be speaking the truth. 'We did, really.'

'Did you lock the door?' said Jack. Susie looked at Binkie – and then she went very red.

'Oh Jack – no, I don't think I did. I was so cross because Peter wouldn't believe me, that I just shoved the telescope into the shed, slammed the door – and ran off with Binkie. I can't remember locking it, or hiding the key.'

'We forgot,' said Binkie, in a very small voice. 'Yes, we forgot. Oh that lovely telescope, Jack! Has it been stolen?'

'I expect so,' said Jack, going back to the telephone. 'Of all the idiots! One of these days, Susie, you'll get into serious trouble. It's just as well it's *our* telescope, not anyone else's.'

He told Peter that Susie and Binkie *had* put back the telescope, but had forgotten to lock the door. Peter was very angry. 'So any prying thief snooping round the shed at night could get in,' he said. 'And of course he'd take the telescope – it would be the most valuable thing there! I'll have to tell my dad, Jack.'

'Oh not just yet!' begged Jack. 'Susie would get into such trouble. I know she's an awful girl, but she *is* my sister, and – well – you know how I feel.'

'Right, Jack. We'll wait till tonight, and see if anything turns up,' said Peter. 'Better have a meeting – half-past five, sharp. But DON'T tell Susie.'

'I won't. But she's so worried and upset that I really don't think she'd even *think* of trying any tricks!' said poor Jack. 'I'm awfully worried too. I know it looks as if Susie and Binkie took the telescope themselves, out of spite – but Susie doesn't tell lies, you know, however annoying she is in other ways.'

'I know she doesn't,' said Peter. 'All right. Five-thirty tonight. I'll tell the others.'

So at half-past five that night a rather subdued Seven met once more down in the old shed. Scamper couldn't *think* what was the matter with them, and ran about wagging his tail and trying to cheer them up.

GOOD OLD SECRET SEVEN

It was a very serious meeting. Everyone already knew about the telescope, because Janet had told the girls in break at school, and Jack and Peter had told George and Colin. Now – what was to be done?

CHAPTER FIFTEEN

EXCITING PLANS

'JACK – you'd better say a few words to everyone about Susie,' said Peter.

So Jack explained how Susie had forgotten to lock the door, and was very, very sorry, and asked the Seven to forgive her and Binkie. 'She says they'll do ANYTHING to help us get it back,' finished Jack. 'I'm most terribly sorry myself – and so thankful that it belonged to me and Susie. I'd have felt dreadful if it had belonged to anyone else.' He felt pretty dreadful now, but *that* would have been just *awful*.

'We're sorry too, Jack,' said Peter. 'And we do believe you when you say that Susie *didn't* take the telescope.'

'I think we ought also to believe her tale of the light that she said she and Binkie saw in the castle last night, when they looked through the telescope,' said Jack, earnestly. 'I know Susie is really most annoying, but *honestly*, Secret Seven, I have never, never once known Susie to tell a lie. She plays jokes, I know, and makes us believe silly things – but she never tells a thumping fib – and if she says she saw a light in the castle last night, then she *did*.'

'I see,' said Peter. 'Well, what do the others say? Do we believe it or not?'

'*I* believe it,' said Pam. 'Susie's an idiot and a nuisance, but I've never known her to tell even a small fib at school to get herself out of trouble. She's too proud to do that. She'd rather take her punishment.'

'Susie's very strong really,' said Barbara, which made everyone look scornfully at her. 'Well, you know what I mean,' she went on. 'She's brave – and bold, and don't-care-ish – and she doesn't cry if she hurts herself, and she'll stick by her friends through thick and thin. In some ways I do admire her, but at times she's just a nuisance.'

This rather remarkable speech by the quiet Barbara surprised everyone.

'I know what you mean, Barbara,' said Janet. 'Let's forgive Susie – and let her help if she wants to.'

But the boys drew the line at that. No – they didn't want Susie's help. Secretly they felt that she might be a bit too clever for them!

'Well – to come back to the point,' said Peter, 'we'll say that we believe what Susie said about seeing a light in the castle – and that means that the woman artist she saw wasn't telling the truth when she said she didn't stay there at night – and it does seem to mean, too, that the light must have been a signal! All right – to whom was she signalling – and why?'

'I think we boys ought to go up to the castle tonight and have another snoop round,' said Colin. 'I feel ashamed now that we ran away as we did! I'd feel better about it if we went up again, and tried to find out what really is going on.'

The other boys nodded. They felt the same. 'But no girls,' said Peter, firmly, seeing that Janet was about to speak. 'NO GIRLS.'

'There's *one* thing we haven't tried to solve,' said George. 'And that is – who on earth stole the telescope! The ordinary thief wouldn't want a thing like that – difficult to sell, and no real use to him! I should have thought he'd have taken the rug off the floor, or our lamp – something like that.'

'Yes, you're right,' said Peter. Then they all jumped as Jack slapped his knee and gave a cry. 'Listen! I bet I know who stole our telescope! *Whoever is hiding in the castle took it!* Susie told that woman artist about the telescope, and how we could see the castle with it, and even saw someone at the window – and if there is any funny business going on up there, that woman would know that our telescope would show it to any of us down here – if we happened to look through it at an awkward moment for them!'

EXCITING PLANS

'So someone popped down here last night, found the shed-door unlocked, went in and stole the telescope so that we couldn't spy on them!' finished Peter. 'Too easy for words! Bother Susie! If only she'd locked the shed, I bet they wouldn't have got in.'

'The thing is – what sort of funny business could be going on, up in the old castle?' wondered Janet. They all frowned and thought hard.

'It would make a really good hiding-place for anything stolen,' suggested Pam. 'Those dungeons would be fine for that.'

'But Susie said there was nothing there but pictures without frames,' said Colin. 'I suppose that woman had painted them, and was storing them there till she could get them framed.'

'Don't be an idiot,' said Jack. 'If there were a lot there, it would have taken anyone *weeks* to paint them. But I tell you what they *might* be! *Old* pictures – valuable ones!'

'Well, they would be framed, if so,' said Barbara.

'Not if they were stolen,' said Jack. 'Nothing easier than to take pictures out of their frames, roll them up, and spirit them away!'

'I think that's rather far-fetched,' objected Janet. 'Honestly I do.'

'All right,' said Jack. 'There's only one thing to do, as far as I can see – and that's to go up there tonight, and watch. Susie said that woman must have been signalling with a light last night. Right – she was presumably signalling to *someone* – probably telling them that the goods were there – they could come and fetch them – or something like that. In which case . . .'

'*Somebody* might go for them tonight!' said George and Colin together.

There was a silence, and everyone thought hard. Then Peter spoke firmly.

'This is what I think our plan should be. We four boys will bike up there again after supper tonight. We will snoop round and see what we can find out. I bet our telescope's hidden up there! If we think we need help, or that Dad ought to know and get busy too, we'll signal with one of our bike lamps. Wave it up and down!'

'Oooh – this is exciting!' said Pam. 'How many times will you wave?'

'Twice if everything's OK, and we can't find anything wrong. Four times if we'd like Dad to come up. More than four times if it's really *urgent*. Got that?'

'Yes,' said everyone, fervently, their eyes shining with excitement.

'Pam and Barbara, you come round after supper and watch with me,' said Janet. 'But wait a minute, Peter – how can we see your signals? We haven't the telescope now, remember, and we can't see any signals without that. The castle is too far away.'

'I've thought of that,' said Peter. 'You must borrow Dad's binoculars – and I think, when we've been gone about half an hour, you'd better tell him the whole story, so that he's ready to come if we need him.'

'This is too exciting for words!' said Pam. 'Binoculars! How clever you are, Peter. Of course, binoculars can see nearly as far as a telescope – they will pick up any signal easily.'

'The meeting is ended,' said Peter, and Scamper got up with a sigh of relief and stretched himself. What a dull meeting – no buns, no biscuits, just talk, talk, talk – and hardly a laugh, and not one single pat! No – Scamper didn't at all approve of meetings like that! He stalked up the path with his tail down.

'Ooooh – twice if it's OK – four times if they want Peter's father to come – and six times if it's urgent!' said Barbara to Pam, as they went home. 'Pam – don't you think that the Secret Seven have a *thrilling* time?'

CHAPTER SIXTEEN

AFTER SUPPER

AFTER SUPPER that night, Peter disappeared to get his bicycle, and to meet the others. 'Now remember, Janet,' he said, as he went out, 'borrow the binoculars and use them – but you needn't ask Dad for them for a while – give us time to get well away, or Dad might come after us, and if there's nothing going on up there, it would be a shame to drag him out when he's tired; but be sure and WATCH FOR ANY SIGNAL.'

'Oh I will, Peter, I will,' said Janet, wishing she was going too. 'Oh, I do so want to come along too. Are you taking Scamper?'

'No. It's too far for him,' said Peter. 'Sorry, Scamper, old thing. Stay home!'

Scamper turned away sadly, tail down again, very miserable. Didn't Peter love him any more? This was the second time that he had gone out without him. Scamper walked down the garden some way behind Peter, wondering where he was going. He watched him take out his bicycle. He saw the other boys come up one by one, and his tail went down even further.

He could bear it no longer when he saw the boys ride off. He would follow them! They would go faster than he could run, but somehow he would smell their trail and follow. 'Wuff,' said Scamper to himself. 'Peter won't know. But I feel as if I MUST be with him tonight!'

And so a lonely figure padded up the road after the bicycles, holding its nose in the air, sniffing, sniffing, trotting away after the four boys. Good old Scamper!

Meantime Janet was watching the clock. She was glad when the two other girls came. Time was going very slowly indeed. She waited until the boys had been gone about half an hour, and then she decided to ask for the binoculars, and tell her parents what was happening! Would they be cross? Well, it couldn't be helped, she must just bear it.

She found the binoculars and went to the sitting-room where her father and mother sat, her mother knitting and her father doing his accounts.

'Dad,' she said. 'May I borrow your binoculars, please?'

'What in the world for?' said her father, astonished. 'At this time of night too!'

And then out everything came – the whole story, higgledy-piggledy at first, so that her parents couldn't make head or tail of what she was telling them. But gradually they understood what had been happening – and why Janet wanted the binoculars!

'Bless us all!' said her father, quite astounded. 'What on earth will you children be up to next? This is a silly business – cycling up to the castle in the dark! As if anything serious could be happening there! Peter's idea of stolen pictures is *nonsense*!'

'Wait a minute, dear,' said his wife. 'I read something in the paper about valuable old paintings being stolen from Lord Lunwood's house – they were cut from their frames – and must have been rolled up and taken away quite easily – in a suitcase, I think the paper said . . .'

Janet gave an excited little scream. 'Oh *Mother* – the pictures Susie and Binkie saw were just rolled up, too – not framed – oh MOTHER!'

And now her parents really did sit up and take notice. They questioned Janet quickly, and were most astonished at all she told them.

'So the four boys have gone up to the castle, all on their own!' said her father. 'This is really a most extraordinary story, Janet, I feel rather worried.'

'You needn't be,' said Janet. 'The boys can look after themselves, Dad – they always have! We can watch for their signal, and see if they need help.'

'I'm not waiting for any signal!' said her father, firmly. 'I'm going up now – and I'm taking Matt the shepherd with me, and the gardener as well!'

'Oh dear!' said Janet. 'We were supposed to wait for a signal. Peter *will* be cross!'

'Well, I shan't mind *that*!' said her father, and went out to get Matt and to tell him to fetch the gardener. They were all to go up in the car.

Janet held the binoculars carefully. Then she suddenly remembered that she hadn't seen Scamper for some time. Wherever is he? she thought. Poor old Scamper! I expect he's sulking in a corner somewhere, because the boys went off without him. I must find him and comfort him!

She went back to where Pam and Barbara were patiently waiting in the playroom for her, and told them quickly what her father was going to do. They whole-heartedly approved.

'Grown-ups always seem to know *at once* what's the best thing to do,' said Pam, thankfully. 'That's one of the differences between them and us! Where are you off to now, Janet?'

'To look for old Scamper,' said Janet. 'Come with me.'

But, of course, they couldn't find Scamper. He was nowhere about, and Janet suddenly felt sure he had gone trailing after the boys. She was very glad.

'Scamper's always a help, anyway,' she said to the others. 'Come on – we'd better go up to the boxroom now and watch for signals through the binoculars. Oh dear – I feel all worked up!'

But though they looked and looked through the binoculars, each taking a turn, no signal came!

'This is awful,' said Janet, when an hour had gone by. 'No "All's Well" signal – and no "Something's Wrong" signal – and no "Urgent" signal – nothing at all! Whatever CAN be happening?'

CHAPTER SEVENTEEN

UP IN THE CASTLE

QUITE A lot had been happening! The boys had set off on their bicycles, all feeling excited. They didn't know that Scamper was padding a long way behind them, sniffing most exciting night-smells as he went. He smelt a hedgehog somewhere in the ditch nearby, but paid no attention. Then he smelt rabbits in the field, and he longed to scatter them. But on he trotted! He was determined to find Peter and see what he was up to. It wasn't fair of Peter to leave him behind!

Peter was now almost at the castle, with the others cycling behind him up the steep hill. How they panted – but as long as *Peter* was still valiantly pedalling, they meant to as well! They were very thankful to see him jump off when he came to the place in the hedge where they had all flung their bicycles before! It had been a hard climb.

'Switch off your lamps,' said Peter. 'I think it will be safe to leave the bikes here. Only the bus comes by usually at night – very few cars.'

They were soon walking cautiously up the grassy hill towards the castle, which loomed above them like a gigantic black shadow. Each of them had a torch, but nobody used one, for fear of warning anybody in the castle. Peter suddenly stopped, not far from the old ruin.

'Go cautiously now,' he commanded. 'In single file – and remember, if trouble comes, one of us must signal with his torch. It doesn't matter which of us – so watch out in case it's necessary.'

They came quietly to the castle. Not a sound was to be heard. It was in complete darkness. When they stepped cautiously inside, their rubber shoes making no sound, a rustling noise began above their heads, and they stopped in fright.

'It's only the roosting jackdaws!' whispered Peter. 'They must have heard our quiet tread! Wait till they settle again.'

Soon there was complete quiet once more. The boys went on down the great hall – and then Peter caught sight of something that made his heart beat quickly.

'Look – there's a light of some sort in that old kitchen-room,' he whispered to the others. 'Stay here. I'm going to see what it is.'

He tiptoed off to the entrance of the huge old room – and stopped in surprise at what he saw. Someone was there – a woman. She had lit a fire of sticks to keep her warm, and it was burning brightly. She was lying on her side, facing the little fire, her eyes closed.

So it was *she* who had stamped out that half-burnt fire we found the other day, the twigs still warm! thought Peter. She must have seen us coming, and hurriedly put it out. I hope she's really *sound* asleep!

She seemed to be. She was lying on a mattress, wrapped all round in rugs (the ones Susie saw down in the dungeons, thought Peter) and didn't move at all. Beside her Peter caught a gleam of a clock's luminous hands, and then his ears picked up its quick ticking.

He tiptoed away and whispered what he had seen to the others. 'She's fast asleep by a fire of twigs. I expect she's here to watch out for anyone coming in the daytime who might discover the secrets of the dungeon. It was really quite a good idea to pretend to be an artist and paint the castle – she could sit all day and keep guard, then!'

'Well, she didn't spot *us* the other day!' said Jack. 'Hey – if she's asleep, I don't think much can be happening tonight, do you? I mean – wouldn't she be awake if somebody was coming in answer to her signal last night?'

'Yes. I suppose she would,' said Peter. 'Oh well – we can at least go down to the dungeons and see if those pictures are there! If they are, we could pick them up and go home with them – then the thieves would have a real shock when they came – they'd find them gone!'

'Good idea!' said George, pleased. 'Let's go down now – but for pity's sake don't let's wake that sleeping woman! Go carefully.'

So, very warily indeed, the four boys went down the old stone dungeon steps. These were much broken and worn, and the boys were glad of their torches to see where they were treading.

'Here we are!' said Peter, when they came at last to the bottom of the steps. 'Whew – what an *awful* place!'

It certainly was! It had great stone walls, black with the dirt of centuries, and the floor was of uneven stone too. Peter shone his torch round and saw great iron staples in the wall.

'I bet plenty of poor wretched prisoners were once roped to those for months – perhaps years,' he said, and everyone shivered at the thought.

'It's not *damp* here, though,' said Jack. 'I thought all dungeons were damp and smelly.'

'Well, this is on a hill, so any water would drain away,' said Peter. 'And, of course, that's why this is a good hiding-place for valuable pictures – it's perfectly dry! Damp would have ruined them at once.'

'Well – where *are* the rolled-up canvases that Susie told us about?' said Jack, flashing his torch all round. 'There's straw here – where maybe tramps rest at times – and some old newspapers – but I can't see much else!'

Jack was right. There were no rolled-up pictures to be found, though they searched everywhere in the great old dungeons.

'Well – I suppose the men have been here already and taken them,' said George, in disappointment.

'Or else Susie made it up!' said Colin. 'Another of her little tricks!'

'No,' said Jack. 'I am certain she didn't make that up. Binkie saw the canvases too, you know. And yet

– if the thieves *have* been to fetch them, why is that woman still here? It must surely mean that she has hidden them somewhere else – maybe because she was afraid that the girls had seen the pictures, and might tell someone.'

'Yes. That's more like it,' said Peter. 'But where can they be hidden? They must be somewhere easy to get at, if the men are coming here for them. They wouldn't want to spend ages getting them out of some difficult hiding-place!'

'Well – there's nothing for it but to do a bit of hunting ourselves!' said Colin. 'Come on! And let's hope we find our telescope somewhere too!'

CHAPTER EIGHTEEN

AN EXCITING DISCOVERY

SO, TREADING very quietly indeed, not daring even to cough, the boys began to look for a likely hiding-place. They hunted in every corner, except in the room where the woman lay asleep, and at last came to the conclusion that the pictures must be somewhere there. It seemed to be the only place left!

'She's probably hidden them under her mattress,' said Peter, with a small groan. 'But let's have one last think. Where would *we* hide them if we had to? And remember, they *could* be straightened out flat.'

Silence. Everyone thought hard. Then Colin whispered loudly: 'I know where *I'd* hide them – under all the mess of twigs the jackdaws have dropped for years, at the base of the big tower!'

'Good idea!' whispered back Peter. 'Fine hiding-place! We'll go and look. Quietly now!' he admonished, as a scramble started.

They tiptoed to where the mass of twigs lay heaped everywhere on the floor, and shone their torches all around. 'It looks as if that pile over there has been messed about a bit,' whispered George, shining his torch on a heaped stack. 'Hold my torch. I'll scrabble about and see.'

He stepped over the masses of twigs, and they cracked loudly beneath his feet. He stopped in a hurry, and waited a moment, afraid that the noise would wake the sleeping woman. Then he leaned forward and began carefully to scrape away the twigs that seemed to have been freshly heaped up.

His hand felt something underneath, and he gave a small cry. 'I believe I've found something!' he whispered, and pulled out what looked rather like a roll of thick paper.

'Yes! It's one of the pictures Susie must have seen down in the dungeons!' said Peter, thrilled. 'See if there are any more.'

Yes – there were plenty more, all neatly rolled up, some of them inside one another. George handed them all out to Peter and Jack. It was a very thrilling moment indeed!

And then they heard something that startled them very much, and made them jump almost out of their skins! A bell! A loud bell that rang and rang and rang, breaking the dark silence so suddenly that the boys felt rooted to the spot. Then the noise stopped, and there was silence again.

'What was it? A telephone bell ringing?' whispered Colin.

'Sounded more like an alarm clock going off,' whispered George, surprised to find himself trembling.

'Of course! It was the clock we heard ticking near that sleeping woman!' said Peter. 'She had set it for a certain time! Maybe the thieves are coming soon, to get the hidden pictures, and she wanted to be sure to be awake. We'd better hide!'

They tiptoed to a small recess in the great wall, and crouched there, their hearts beating fast. Peter and Jack had the rolled-up pictures. They waited there, quite silent.

They heard movements after a minute or two, and then the light of a lamp came from the kitchen-like room where the woman had been sleeping. The light came nearer, and the crouching boys saw the woman pass their recess, holding the light before her to see the way. They huddled in the dark shadows, hardly daring to breathe!

She passed right by, went to the great entrance, and stood there. 'She's signalling!' whispered Peter. 'I bet that's to say "All's Clear – come and get the goods"!'

'Oh goodness! The girls at home will see the signal and think it's *ours*!' groaned Jack. 'I wonder how many times that woman's waving.'

'Let's get out of here,' said Colin. 'I don't want to be found by whoever's coming up to the castle. Let's go now, whilst we've time.'

'Well, we should have plenty of time, if the thieves have to come from any distance,' said Peter. 'But maybe they're hiding somewhere near, so we'll have to look out! Come on – we'll rush by that woman – she *will* have a fright! Let's hope we can signal with our torches when we get out on the hillside!'

They all left the dark little recess and raced to the entrance, where the woman stood, the lamp still in her hand. She gave a scream when they pushed past her, and tried to catch hold of Colin.

'Stop! Who are you? Stop, I say!'

But the boys did not stop. They tore out into the darkness. Then Peter had a shock – he tripped over something and fell headlong – and down went all the others too! Before they could get up, firm hands had hold of them, and each boy was pulled roughly to his feet. A bright torch was shone into their faces.

'Kids!' said a man's voice. 'Four boys! What on earth are you doing here, I'd like to know!'

Three men stood there, dark shadows in the night, lit only by the torch they held towards the four boys. They had neatly tripped each of them as they came racing out into the darkness.

'Let me go!' yelled Peter, and kicked out hard. The man holding him tightened his grip.

'Quite a little spitfire,' he said, mockingly, and shook him hard. The woman came up, then, amazed.

'I've not seen them before,' she said. 'They must have been hiding in the castle.'

'Are the things safe?' said the tallest man, sharply.

'I'll see,' she said, and went off. The boys waited, their hearts thumping. They knew that the pictures were certainly *not* safe in their hiding-place. No – they were well down the hillside now, where they had rolled after Peter and Jack had kicked them, as soon as the men caught hold of their arms. How they hoped that nobody had seen the rolls of pictures bumping down the hillside in the darkness!

The woman came hurrying back. 'They're gone!' she said. 'Not a single one there. These boys must have taken them and hidden them somewhere! Whatever made them come here! They *couldn't* have known anything about them!'

'We'll soon find out,' said the tall man. 'Shove the boys into the dungeons and keep them there till they tell us what they are doing here at this time of night – and where they've put the pictures!'

And then, very roughly indeed, the four boys were pushed into the castle, and down into the dungeons! What a horrible thing to happen, just as they had been about to go home in triumph!

CHAPTER NINETEEN

A FRIEND IN NEED!

'OH NO! This is a sickening thing to happen!' said Peter, rubbing himself where he had fallen against the hard stone floor. 'What bad luck to run headlong into those men!'

'Peter! What happened to the pictures?' said George, in a whisper.

'We managed to drop them and give them a good kick down the hill,' answered Peter. 'I hope they're still rolling!'

'What are we going to do?' asked Colin, who felt decidedly scared.

'I don't see that we can do *anything* at the moment,' said Peter. 'What a pity we weren't able to signal to the girls, after all! Then we'd know help was coming.'

'What do you suppose those men are doing?' asked George. 'Looking for the pictures?'

'I should think so,' said Peter. 'They'll be down here soon enough, when they can't find them anywhere!'

Nobody liked hearing that! Their hearts sank. Peter began to wonder if he could possibly get out of the castle and signal home. No. He couldn't. One of the men would be sure to be watching at the top of the dungeon steps.

And then something most astonishing happened! There was no *man* at the top of the steps – only the woman, who had been told to shout if the boys tried to escape. Quite suddenly the boys heard her give a scream, and then she shouted, 'Oh, what is it, what is it?'

Then something bounded down the steps at top speed, and flung itself on top of Peter, whining in delight!

'*Scamper!*' cried Peter, in the utmost astonishment. 'Whatever are *you* doing here? How did you find us?

Oh good dog, clever dog! Oh, how glad I am to see you!'

Scamper whined and barked and licked every one of the boys. What a long, long trek he had had, following their trail – but now, here he was, *just* at the right moment! He leapt up at Peter, and went almost mad with joy.

The boys felt braver at once. Scamper would be a real help! The woman's screams had brought the men up at once, and they shouted to her.

'What's happening? What is it?'

'Oh, something pushed by me in the dark and shot down into the dungeon!' she said. 'It *seemed* to be a dog!'

Scamper immediately produced an extremely fierce growl down at the bottom of his throat – it startled even Peter, who was used to Scamper's barks and growls.

'Urrrrr. URRRRRR, URRRRRRR!

'You be careful of our dog!' yelled Peter. 'He'll attack you if you don't let us go.'

'You tell us where you've put those pictures and we'll let you go all right,' came back the angry answer. 'Otherwise we'll keep you here for a week!'

'Rubbish!' shouted back Peter. 'Our people will soon come after us. *We* don't mind staying here. Makes a nice change!'

All the same, the boys didn't at all like being down in the dungeons. They were dark and full of shadows – and they were very cold indeed! One of the men decided to give the boys a scare and came rushing down the steps, hallooing at the top of his voice. He certainly startled the boys – but as he also had the effect of making Scamper go wild with rage, it didn't do him much good! The spaniel flew at him, and nipped him smartly on the leg. The man gave a howl and went up the steps as quickly as he had come down!

'Good dog, Scamper,' said Peter, pleased. 'Gosh, I'm glad you trailed us tonight! What a long walk you've had, old fellow! You're a really good friend!'

For about an hour nothing happened. What were the men doing? Having a meal? Looking for the pictures? Nobody could guess. They all felt very thankful that Scamper was there to protect them.

'We wouldn't have had a chance without him!' said Peter. Then he stiffened as he heard a distant noise. 'Listen – something's going on! Listen to that shouting and yelling!'

They listened – and Scamper suddenly gave a delighted whine and tore up the stone steps at top speed.

'Hey, come back!' yelled Peter – but Scamper took no notice.

'Let's go and see what's happening,' said Peter, and started up the steps. 'There can't be anyone guarding us now, if Scamper shot away like that.'

They all went cautiously up the steps – and, as Peter said, there was no one on guard at the top. But outside the castle there was certainly *something* going on! Shouts and yells and the sound of feet stamping about – what a to-do! Scamper was in the midst of it, barking and nipping whenever he had a chance! Quick, Peter – where's your torch?

CHAPTER TWENTY

SAFE HOME AGAIN!

PETER SHONE his torch on to the shouting mob – and nearly dropped it in surprise. 'DAD! How did *you* get here! And *Matt*! Hey, look – there's Dad and Matt and the gardener – and they've caught all three of the men!'

The torches shone on the six men and the excited dog. There was no sign of the woman – she had fled away while she had the chance!

'Now then – you just come along quietly,' said Matt's deep voice. The big shepherd was having the time of his life! He could handle bulls and cows and horses and rams and goodness knows what – and he had no difficulty at all in handling two or three frightened men, especially with Peter's father and the hefty gardener to help.

SAFE HOME AGAIN!

'Dad! Oh Dad! How did you know we wanted help – we weren't able to signal!' cried Peter, as his father neatly pinioned his man's arms behind him.

'Hallo, Peter – so you're all right!' said his father. 'We're just taking these men down to their van to lock them in and Matt will drive them down to the police station. I'm sure the police will give them a bed tonight! We found their van parked up the lane, ready to take them off again – with the pictures too, I suppose! We saw your bikes somewhere down the lane as well!'

'Oh *Dad*! I can't believe you're here!' said Peter, full of thankfulness. 'I suppose Janet told you where we were. Can we do anything to help you with these men?'

'No – but you might look around for those pictures,' said his father. 'They're too valuable to be left in the damp and cold. These fellows won't tell us where they are.'

'Perhaps that woman took them,' suggested Matt, marching the tall man away in front of him. 'She scuttled off like a rabbit.'

'No – she didn't take them,' said Peter. '*I* know where they are! I'll get them!'

He and the others raced down the hill with their torches to find where the rolled-up pictures had gone. Now – where were they? Surely that woman hadn't found them? No – there they were, lying where they had rolled, safe and sound, spread all about the hillside!

'Good!' said Peter, and pounced on them. Soon he and the boys had gathered them all, and ran back to where the men were now being bundled into their own van. They stared angrily when they saw the rolls of canvases carried by the boys.

Matt drove away in the van, with the three angry, frightened men locked inside. Peter's father and the gardener went to the car in which they had driven up.

'You boys will come down on your bikes, won't you?' Peter's father shouted. 'What about Scamper?'

'Oh take him in the car, Dad, if you will,' said Peter, lifting up the excited dog. 'He walked all the way here, dear old fellow – he must be tired now!'

Scamper was thankful to go back in the car. Peter's father carefully put the precious canvases out of his reach, and away they went down the hill, following the van.

What a joyful meeting the Seven had in Peter's playroom, as soon as they arrived back. The girls and Peter's mother gave them a great welcome and could hardly wait to hear their news – and how eagerly they listened to the four boys' exciting story.

'Oh *what* a time you had!' said Janet, her eyes shining. 'Oh, I *wish* I'd been with you! Whatever will Susie and Binkie say when they hear all this? By the way, did you find our telescope in the castle? I suppose the men had hidden it somewhere there?'

'No – we didn't find the telescope!' said Jack. 'Bother! We ought to have asked those men where it was – our marvellous telescope that brought us this exciting adventure!'

'Here's Dad back again,' said Peter, hearing the front door open, and Scamper's loud barking as he too came in, and rushed up the stairs. Peter opened the playroom door, and Scamper jumped up at him in joy.

'Dad! We're all up here, Mother too!' called Peter. 'Oh Dad – THANK you for coming to our rescue! We couldn't even give the signal for help – so we'd all be down in those miserable dungeons still, if you hadn't rescued us. Oh Dad – wasn't it exciting!'

'Excuse me,' said Jack, anxiously, 'did the men say anything about my telescope? We're pretty sure they stole it because they knew we were watching the castle through it.'

'Oh yes – they've admitted that they stole it,' said Peter's father. 'But I'm sorry to have to tell you that they didn't take it up to the castle – they simply threw it away into the river.'

'Oh my goodness!' said Jack, looking very down in the dumps. 'That's a blow. It was such a *wonderful* telescope – I'll never, never have another like it.'

'You will, old chap!' said Peter's father. 'There's a reward offered for those pictures – a pretty good one too – and as it will go to the Secret Seven of course, I'm sure that at their next meeting they will agree to buying you a *magnificent* telescope, Jack – and there will be enough money over for the Seven to save for a very good Christmas, as well – you certainly deserve it!'

'And Scamper, you shall have the *biggest* bone we can buy you!' said Janet, patting the spaniel's silky head. 'Oh I'm longing for our next Secret Seven meeting – we'll have such plans to make!'

You will, Janet! How we'd like to listen in and hear your excited voices, planning how to spend that reward – a fine new telescope for Jack and Susie – a bone for Scamper – a lovely Christmas for everyone. And I'm sure we can all guess what your *next* password will be – PICTURES! Are we right, Peter?

**Read on for more stories
and fun facts about
THE SECRET SEVEN!**

ABOUT THE SECRET SEVEN

The Secret Seven Society consists of Peter, his sister Janet, and their friends Jack, Colin, George, Pam and Barbara. Peter and Janet's golden spaniel Scamper also attends meetings, which are held in a shed with S.S. on the door. Admission is by password only and badges must be worn. Peter, as head of the society, makes sure that everyone follows the rules!

The Seven puzzle over strange goings-on in their local community, aiming to solve mysteries and put things right. Their work often involves hiding and keeping watch, hunting for clues, shadowing suspicious characters and questioning people. Burglaries, stolen animals and missing children feature in various stories – as do fireworks, a tree-house, a telescope and Susie's toy aeroplane.

The first of the fifteen Secret Seven books was published in 1949, with the final title appearing in 1963. However, Peter and Janet had appeared in an earlier book called *At Seaside Cottage* (1947) and the story of the formation of the society had been told in the short story Secret of the Old Mill (1948.) There are five other Secret Seven short stories, which are gathered together in *The Secret Seven Short Story Collection*.

Enid Blyton rewrote the Secret Seven stories so they could be adapted into cartoons. These were published in the *Mickey Mouse Weekly* in 1951. They were illustrated by George Brook, who was one of the original illustrators of the series.

A Secret Seven card game was launched in 1955 and in 1954, four Secret Seven jigsaw puzzles appeared from Bestime. Whitman released four new jigsaw puzzles in 1975. In the 1970s, Evelyne Lallemand wrote a 12-book series of Secret Seven continuation books in French, nine of which were translated into English by Anthea Bell between 1983 and 1987, but they are long out of print. Between 1978 and 1984, the Secret Seven could be found in annuals.

LET'S HAVE A CLUB OF OUR OWN – PART THREE

*Now that we have a location for the meetings, and we know who's in the club, it's time to think of that all-important name. If you've missed out on the story so far, then look in the back of **Puzzle for the Secret Seven** and **Secret Seven Fireworks** and you'll soon be up to speed …*

'Well, thanks awfully for voting me leader,' said Mark. 'I'll do my best to be a decent one. Now then – let's choose the name for our club. The "something" Six – what shall it be?'

Ideas came quickly, and were shouted out eagerly. 'The Strong Six! The Striking Six! The Shocking Six! The Trusty Six! The Secret Six!'

'Not the Secret Six. Too much like the well-known Secret Seven,' said Mark. 'Let's have a definite name of our own.'

'The Stalwart Six! The Sturdy Six!' cried Eric. 'The …'

'Wait! What about the *Sturdy* Six?' said Mark. 'Seems a good, strong sort of name to me. To be sturdy is to be trustable and straight and dependable and strong – "The Sturdy Six" – yes, that seems a good name to me for our club. Hands up those who like it best of all the names.'

Every hand went up. Mark nodded. 'Right – I hereby proclaim that we six are now formed into a club which has the name of the Sturdy Six.'

Mollie grinned round in delight. 'Mark's a good leader already!' she remarked. 'I hereby proclaim that he is a ...'

'Shut up, please, Mollie,' said Mark. 'Now about badges. We shall need to have S.S. on them, for Sturdy Six. Er – any suggestions?'

The four boys gazed hard at the two girls, and they at once responded! 'All right – we know what those looks mean!' said Mollie. 'You want us to make the badges for us all. Right, we will!'

'How will you make them?' asked James.

'Easy!' said Katie. 'We'll get six buttons all the same size. We'll cut out bits of cloth, and embroider S.S. on them for Sturdy Six. Then we'll sew each bit over the button, so that the S.S. is on the front – and sew a little safety-pin on the back to pin the badge on to our coats. S.S. for the Sturdy Six – shan't we be proud to wear them?'

'Thanks awfully,' said Mark. 'Now for a password. Any suggestions?'

There were plenty! 'Hen-house!' said Eric, looking round at the perches.

'New laid eggs,' said Katie, and everyone chuckled.

'Sturdy!' said Mark.

'Cluck-cluck!' said Mollie. That made everyone laugh so much that it was chosen at once for the password.

'Whatever will people think when they hear us murmuring "cluck-cluck" to each other when we meet?' said Katie.

'Well, it's really only a password to gain entrance to our meeting-place,' said Mark. 'In future, no one can enter any of our meetings, wherever they are, unless he or she first says the password. So don't forget it, please.'

'Shall we discuss a secret signal now?' asked Dick, but Mark was looking at his watch. He shook his head.

'Sorry – the meeting's over. Meet here on Friday evening at half past five again. We'll then discuss what our aim should be, what things we can do together, and a secret signal if we think it's necessary. Buck up – it's time to go if we're going to get any homework done this evening!'

They all trooped out of the hen-house, feeling thrilled and pleased. 'I'm glad you're leader, Mark,' said Eric. 'You can direct everything well, that's quite plain. Well – the Sturdy Six are now a club – and I'm jolly glad to belong to it!'

Hooray for the Sturdy Six! Now, find a copy of **Shock for the Secret Seven** *to find out what happened next.*

Let's Have a Club of Our Own © Hodder & Stoughton, 1953

THE LIFE AND TIMES OF ENID BLYTON

1940S

The Second World War raged through Europe and other parts of the world in the 1940s. Many everyday items were rationed – including paper (which was rationed until 1949). But Enid kept writing and had a very successful decade . . .

September, 1940   Enid publishes *The Naughtiest Girl in the School* - the first in a series of three books, and the first of Enid's school stories.

November   First two books under the pseudonym of Mary Pollock published. (Enid used several made-up names throughout her career.)

The Children of Cherry Tree Farm is published, and is the first full-length purpose-written book that turns into a series.

Old Thatch is sold.

1941 Enid publishes eight books including *The Adventurous Four*, and *The Twins at St Clare's* – the first in a series of six books. Enid publishes her first calendar, *Sunny Stories Calendar* 1942.

1942 Publishes 22 books including *Enid Blyton's Readers* 1–3. These books were the first to feature her now famous logo-signature (which you can see on the front of this book), and were Enid's first collaboration with Eileen Soper.

September   *Five on a Treasure Island* – the first of a series of 21 books about the Famous Five were published

December   Enid's marriage to Hugh ends in divorce, and the following October, she marries Kenneth Darrell Waters.

1943   Publishes 23 books including *The Mystery of the Burnt Cottage*, the first of the Find-Outers Mysteries - a series of 15 books and *The Children's Life of Christ*, her first book re-telling tales from the Bible.

1944   Publishes 24 books in this year including the first of the eight 'Adventure' books, *The Island of Adventure*.

March, 1945   Enid's first appearance in *Playways*, with 'The Caravan Family'. In September, Enid began writing for *Good Housekeeping* – to which she contributed regularly until August 1948

November 14   Last 'Letter from Green Hedges' in *Teachers World*.

July 1946   *First Term at Malory Towers* published - the first in a series of six books.

November, 1948 *Enid Blyton Diary* published.

Also in 1948 came the first four Enid Blyton character jigsaws from Bestime, and 'Journey Through Fairyland,' the first Enid Blyton board game.

1949 Enid releases 32 books this year, including the first of the six Barney Mysteries, called *The Rockingdown Mystery*.

June 5 Noddy makes his first appearance in the *Sunday Graphic*, and in November appears in book form in *Noddy Goes to Toyland*.

May 21 Enid's first contribution to the *Evening Standard*. She kept writing for the paper until December 1953.

November   *The Secret Seven* - the first 'proper book' in a series of 15 books is published.

This timeline continues in the next Secret Seven title . . .

SECRET SEVEN PASSWORDS

Have you noticed how important passwords are to the Secret Seven? Here's a complete list of them, book by book. Which passwords would you use for your own club? Why not make a list?

1. The Secret Seven

Wenceslas

Weekdays

2. Secret Seven Adventure

Rabbits

Indians

Adventure

3. Well Done, Secret Seven

Adventure

4. Secret Seven on the Trail

Picked Onions

Cheeky Charlie

5. Go Ahead Secret Seven

Jack Sprat

Beware

6. Good Work Secret Seven

Guy Fawkes

Fireworks

7. Secret Seven Win Through

Easter Egg

Thursday

8. Three Cheers Secret Seven

Lollipops

Grim

9. Secret Seven Mystery

Mint Sauce

Stable Boy

10. Puzzle for the Secret Seven

Wuff

Thump

11. Secret Seven Fireworks

Wee Willie Winkie

Cheeky Charile

12. Good Old Secret Seven

Wuff-Wuff

Telescope

13. Shock for the Secret Seven

Toad in the Hole

14. Look Out, Secret Seven

Holidays

15. Fun for the Secret Seven

Scamper

HOW WELL DO YOU REMEMBER GOOD OLD SECRET SEVEN?

Here are questions to test your memory. The answers are printed on the next page, but they're upside down. No cheating!

1. What present did Jack get from Uncle Bob?

2. Which of the Secret Seven sees a man in the old castle tower?

3. How do the Secret Seven try to prevent Susie from following them to the castle?

4. How do the Seven know that someone has been in the castle very recently?

5. What frightens Pam?

6. How did Susie and Binkie get to the castle?

7. Who did they meet when they arrived there?

8. What item do Peter and Janet have to borrow from their father?

9. What is the signal the boys agree to make if they need help?

10. Who follows the boys on their adventure?

11. Where in the castle are the missing pictures hidden?

12. Where are the boys kept prisoner?

1. A telescope. 2. Janet. 3. They leave half an hour later. 4. The firewood they find is still warm. 5. She hears someone wailing in the dungeons. 6. They took the bus. 7. An artist. 8. His binoculars. 9. They will wave their bike lamps six times. 10. Scamper the dog. 11. Under the pile of jackdaw twigs. 12. In the castle dungeons.

START YOUR
SECRET SEVEN CLUB

In each of the Tony Ross editions of The Secret Seven is a Club Token (see below).
Collect any five tokens and you'll get a brilliant Secret Seven club pack –
perfect for you and your friends to start your very own secret club!

GET THE SECRET SEVEN CLUB PACK:

7 club pencils   **7 club bookmarks**   **1 club poster**   **7 club badges**

Simply fill in the form below, send it in with your
five tokens, and we'll send you the club pack!

Send to:

**Secret Seven Club, Hachette Children's Books,
Marketing Department, 338 Euston Road, London NW1 3BH**

Closing date: 31st December 2013

TERMS AND CONDITIONS:
(1) Open to UK and Republic of Ireland residents only (2) You must provide the email address of a parent or guardian for your entry to be valid (3) Photocopied tokens are not accepted (4) The form must be completed fully for your entry to be valid (5) Club packs are distributed on a first come, first served basis while stocks last (6) No part of the offer is exchangeable for cash or any other offer (7) Please allow 28 days for delivery (8) Your details will only be used for the purposes of fulfilling this offer and, if you choose [see tick box below], to send email newsletters about Enid Blyton and other great Hachette Children's books, and will never be shared with any third party.

✂ -

Please complete using capital letters (UK Residents Only)

**I SECRET SEVEN
CLUB TOKEN**

FIRST NAME:

SURNAME:

DATE OF BIRTH: DD | MM | YYYY

ADDRESS LINE 1:

ADDRESS LINE 2:

ADDRESS LINE 3:

POSTCODE:

PARENT OR GUARDIAN'S EMAIL ADDRESS:

☐ I'd like to receive a regular Enid Blyton email newsletter and information
about other great Hachette Children's books (I can unsubscribe at any time).

www.thesecretseven.co.uk

THE SECRET SEVEN ONLINE

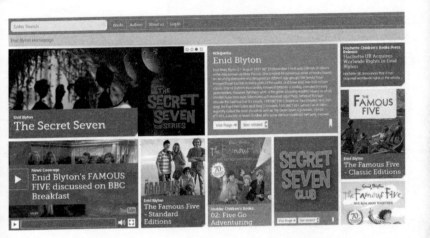

ON THE WEBSITE, YOU CAN:-

- Download and make your very own **SECRET SEVEN** door hanger
- Get tips on how to set up your own **SECRET SEVEN** club
- Find **SECRET SEVEN** snack recipes for your own club meetings
- Take the **SECRET SEVEN** quiz to see how much you really know!

Sign up to get news of brilliant competitions and more great books

AND MUCH MORE!

GO TO ... WWW.THESECRETSEVEN.CO.UK AND JOIN IN!

Enid Blyton

CELEBRATE 70 YEARS OF

The Famous Five

These special edition jackets of the first five books have been brought to you by Quentin Blake and friends in support of the House of Illustration.

CHRIS RIDDELL

OLIVER JEFFERS

Quentin Blake

Helen Oxenbury

Emma Chichester Clark

Also available as an ebook

www.famousfivebooks.com
www.houseofillustration.org.uk

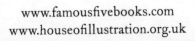

Elizabeth Allen is spoilt, mischievous and determined
to get home – whatever the cost – she really is the
Naughtiest Girl in the school! Exciting stories about
the girls and boys boarding at Whyteleafe School.

For the full range of Naughtiest Girl books and eBooks, please see
www.hodderchildrens.co.uk

Hodder
Children's
Books